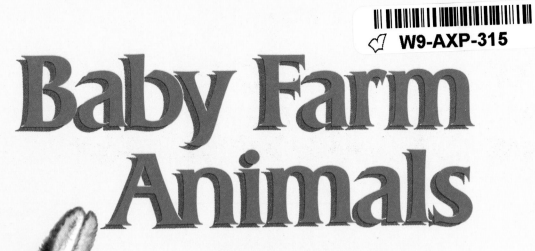

Baby Farm Animals

Illustrated by Garth Williams

A GOLDEN BOOK • NEW YORK

Western Publishing Company, Inc.
Racine, Wisconsin 53404

Copyright © 1959, 1953 Western Publishing Company, Inc. All rights reserved. Printed in the U.S.A. No part of this book may be reproduced or copied in any form without written permission from the publisher. GOLDEN®, GOLDEN & DESIGN®, and A GOLDEN BOOK® are trademarks of Western Publishing Company, Inc. ISBN 0-307-10393-5/ISBN 0-307-60845-X (lib. bdg.)   C D E F G H I J

BABY CATS are called kittens. They love playing on the farm. At night the farmer gives them fresh cow's milk, and the kittens curl up together in the big red barn.

BABY RABBIT lives in a hutch, which is his little house. He hops through the grass every morning to see his friends the guinea pigs.

BABY GUINEA PIGS have come out of their hutch to nibble leaves for breakfast. They are glad to see their friend the rabbit.

BABY DONKEY is sitting down because
he is tired. Someone is trying to make him
stand up and follow those juicy carrots tied
on the end of a stick.

But Baby Donkey knows that trick and he
does not get up.

BABY DUCKS are called ducklings. They swim in the pond with their wide, webbed feet.

"Why don't you come for a swim?" they ask the chicks.

BABY CHICKENS are called chicks. They cannot swim.

"Mother says we must look for seeds and stay out of the water," they reply.

BABY PIG is called a piglet. He loves to sleep on clean straw. A piglet digs with his nose, which is called a snout. If someone picks him up or chases him, he will squeal for his mother.

BABY COW is called a calf. She says, "Moooo," whenever she wants her mother and some milk. When she was only a few hours old, she could go for a walk in the pasture and eat grass, daisies, and dandelions.

BABY DOG is called a puppy. He thinks he is big and strong. He growls and barks at strangers. He pretends that the shoe is a big cat, and he growls and barks at it, too.

BABY SHEEP is called a lamb. He is crying
for his mother: "Baa, baa, baa!" If he looks in the
barn, he will find her. When the lamb grows up,
he will have a thick coat of curly wool.

BABY GOATS are called kids. They are frisky and playful. They try to knock each other down by butting their heads together.

BABY SWANS are called cygnets. They are covered with soft, smoke-colored down. When they grow up, they will have pure white feathers and long, long necks.

BABY GEESE are called goslings. They will be big gray geese someday. One gosling is dipping her head under the water. She is looking for something to eat.

BABY HORSE is called a foal. She could walk the day she was born. Now, after a week, she gallops. When she is two years old, she will be a beautiful horse, and she will be able to carry a rider on her back.

Perhaps she will win a race.